SCOOBY-DOO!™
Museum
MADNESS

by Jesse Leon McCann

SCHOLASTIC INC.

New York   Toronto   London   Auckland   Sydney
Mexico City   New Delhi   Hong Kong   Buenos Aires

visit us at www.abdopublishing.com • Reinforced library bound edition published in 2012 by Spotlight, a division of the ABDO Group, 8000 West 78th Street, Edina, Minnesota 55439. Spotlight produces high-quality reinforced library bound editions for schools and libraries. Published by agreement with Warner Bros.—A Time Warner Company. The stories, characters, and incidents mentioned are entirely fictional. All rights reserved. Used under authorization. Printed in the United States of America, Melrose Park, Illinois. • 052011• 092011
♻This book contains at least 10% recycled materials.

 Copyright © 2011 Hanna-Barbera. SCOOBY-DOO and all related characters and elements are trademarks of and © Hanna-Barbera. WB SHIELD: ™ & © Warner Bros. Entertainment Inc. (s11)

Library of Congress Cataloging-in-Publication Data
This title was previously cataloged with the following information:
McCann, Jesse Leon.
   Museum madness / by Jesse Leon McCann ; cover and interior illustrations, Duendes Del Sur.
-- Reinforced library bound ed.
       p. cm. -- (Scooby-Doo)
   The Coolsville Museum is throwing a party to celebrate their newest exhibit when an uninvited mummy shows up looking for revenge.
   1. Scooby-Doo (Fictitious character)--Juvenile fiction 2. Mummies --Juvenile fiction. 3. Dogs --Juvenile Fiction.
   4. Museums --Fiction. 5. Mystery and detective stories.
PZ7.M1247 Mu 2008
[E]--dc22
                                      2008301050
ISBN 978-1-59961-867-8 (reinforced library bound edition)

Scooby-Doo and his pals from Mystery, Inc. were invited to a fancy party at the Coolsville Museum. It was to celebrate a new exhibit — the tomb of an ancient Egyptian king!

"Welcome, everyone!" announced museum curator Lotta Kayre. "Enjoy yourselves tonight, that is, unless King Shaggunkamen's *curse* gets you first!"

THE MYSTERIOUS
TREASURES OF KIN

SHAGGUNKAME

While Shaggy and Scooby chowed down at the party, Fred, Daphne, and Velma mingled in the crowd.

"*I'm* the cursed one!" artist Pierce Deere complained to Daphne. "My exhibit was canceled, thanks to this mummy thing!"

4

"Humph! One shouldn't mock a curse — it might come true," Lord Dusty Diggs, a famous Egyptologist, told Velma. "In fact, they shouldn't have removed King Shagg's sarcophagus from the pyramid at all!"

"I wanted to buy King Shaggunkamen's treasures for my personal collection," Iona Bunch, Coolsville's richest citizen, explained to Fred. "But the museum wouldn't sell! 'The treasure's for everyone to enjoy!' they said. Can you imagine?"

Shaggy dropped an egg roll, and it bounced across the floor. "Come back here, little eggy-roll. Like, I'm gonna gobble you up!" Shaggy called.

Scooby saw Shaggy going into an area that was off-limits. "*Ruh-oh!*"

Scooby didn't like it inside of the exhibit. It was too dark and spooky. He liked it even less when a long, bony arm grabbed him from behind.

"Rooooooh!"

7

It was just Shaggy! Shaggy had found some old stuff somewhere and dressed up like the ancient pharaoh.

"Like, chill out, Scoob," said Shaggy. "Look at that statue of the ol' king! He looks just like me!"

Scooby-Doo wanted to get back to the party. He didn't like tombs or ancient curses!

DANGER!
Do Not
Open Tomb!

Shaggy insisted they go into the sarcophagus room. Scooby-Doo gulped when he saw where Shaggy had found his pharaoh's outfit — in the king's ancient crypt! The cursed crypt!

Shaggy didn't notice. He was too busy admiring his reflection, "Yep! I'm the spitting image of ol' King Shaggunkamen!"

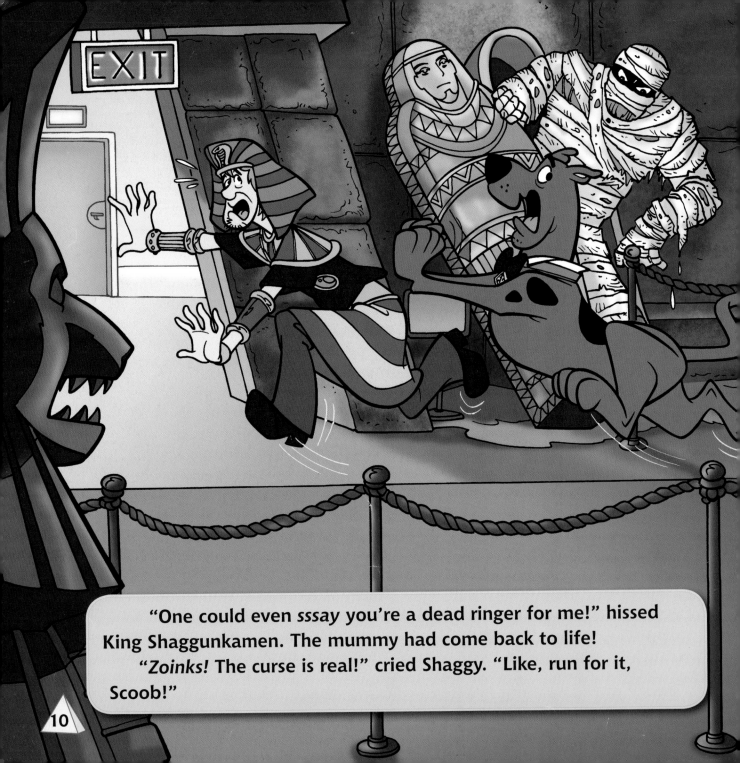

"One could even *sssay* you're a dead ringer for me!" hissed King Shaggunkamen. The mummy had come back to life!
"*Zoinks!* The curse is real!" cried Shaggy. "Like, run for it, Scoob!"

Shaggy and Scooby ran as fast as they could. "How dare you defile my tomb!" King Shagg hissed in a high-pitched voice. "*Ssseize* them, my minions!"

"Relp!" Scooby yelled. "Rummies!" Just as more mummies came after them, Scooby and Shaggy found an emergency exit. A loud alarm went off when they ran through the doors. *Wee-Ooo-Wee-Ooo!*

The party-goers ran from the museum. Some people had heard the emergency alarm, and some people had seen the ghoulish mummies!

"My exhibit is ruined!" cried Lotta, the museum curator.

"Like, it's the mummy's curse!" Shaggy said.

"There's no such thing as curses," said Fred. "I think we've got another mystery on our hands."

The Mystery, Inc. gang went back into the museum to check out the exhibit. It wasn't long before they were attacked by the growling mummies.

"Grrrwarr!"

Crash!

"*Jinkies!* Look out!" Velma hollered. "These guys have some serious anger issues!"

The gang escaped the mummies and searched King Shaggunkamen's tomb for clues.

"Look at these pearls!" Velma exclaimed. "It looks like they're from Iona Bunch's necklace."

"And there's Lord Diggs' cummerbund," Daphne pointed. *"Jeepers! Is he behind all this?"*

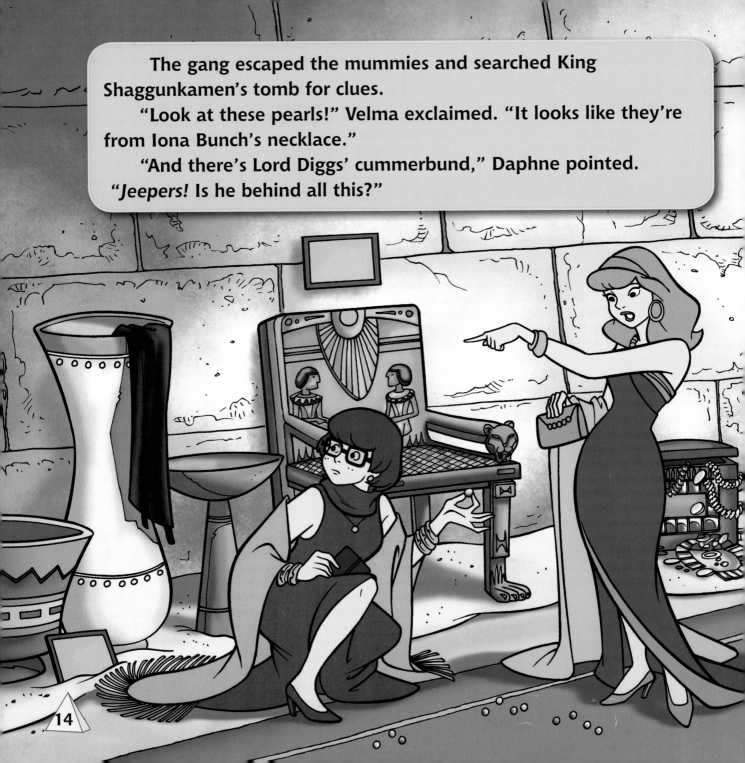

"Like, check out at this groovy earring," Shaggy said. "I think I saw that grouchy artist wearing it."

"Reah! Rouchy!" Scooby nodded.

"We've got to get a close-up look at those mummies to learn more," Fred said. "Shaggy and Scooby, I'll need your help."

15

Shaggy and Scooby didn't like Fred's plan, but after a few Scooby Snacks, they agreed to do it. Daphne and Velma spread guacamole on Shaggy, so he looked more like the ancient King Shaggunkamen. And Scooby put on the head of a broken statue.

"Like, hey there, uh, my minions," Shaggy said to the mummies. "Like, it's me, ol' King Shaggy-carpet."

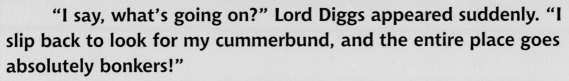

"I say, what's going on?" Lord Diggs appeared suddenly. "I slip back to look for my cummerbund, and the entire place goes absolutely bonkers!"

"My *curssse* is unleashed and you are doomed!" cried King Shaggunkamen, coming out of the shadows.

"My stars!" exclaimed Lord Diggs as he nearly fainted from fear.

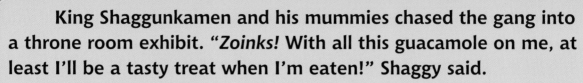

King Shaggunkamen and his mummies chased the gang into a throne room exhibit. *"Zoinks!* With all this guacamole on me, at least I'll be a tasty treat when I'm eaten!" Shaggy said.

Suddenly, a stone tile gave way under the gang and they fell through the floor!

"Rooooh nooooo!" cried Scooby.

Things went from bad to worse! The gang landed in a dusty chamber filled with dangerous snakes, spiders, and creepy, crawly insects. But they weren't the only unexpected visitors!

"Help! I fell through a hole and got stuck in this vase!" It was the artist, Pierce Deere. "Don't just stand there, get me out!" But the gang had more important things to worry about!

"Wait a minute! These snakes are fakes," Velma said.

It was true. The snakes, spiders, and insects were all made of rubber! The gang helped Pierce get unstuck, but he thought they'd played a prank on him, "I'm sure you think this was really funny! Well, *ha-ha.*" He left in a huff.

"*Hmm.* That urn Pierce was stuck in gives me another idea," Fred said.

Scooby-Doo and Shaggy were enlisted again to get the attention of the mummies, who chased them up some steps. Suddenly, Shaggy and Scooby turned on King Shaggunkamen and his minions and threw rubber snakes and other creepy-crawlies at them!

"*Eeeek!* Snakes and insects!" King Shagg said in a high-pitched voice. "Get them away! Get them away!"

The frightened mummies fell backward down the stairs. Daphne, Fred, and Velma caught them in Egyptian urns. Fred's plan worked!

The gang rolled the urns back to the sarcophagus room to unmask the villains.

"It's Iona Bunch and her bodyguards," Velma exclaimed. "She must have broken her pearl necklace as she changed into her King Shaggunkamen disguise."

"I figured if I convinced everyone the treasure was really cursed, they'd sell it to me," Iona sneered. "I would have gotten away with it, if it hadn't been for you meddling kids and your dog!"

The next morning, the gang returned to the museum to make sure the exhibit's opening day went smoothly. Lotta Kayre, the curator, thanked the gang for all their help.

"The exhibit is a great success, and I owe it all to you and Scooby-Doo!" Lotta smiled.

"*Scooby-dooby-doo!*" cheered Scooby-Doo.